PUFFIN BOOKS
Magic in the Air

'Magic broomstick indeed! You should know
better,' said Mr Robson, the schoolmaster,
scornfully, and he went quickly back into the
house.

So it was only Sam who watched the
Weathervane Witch on the school roof hitch up
her billowing black skirt and fly off on her
broomstick to tell her friend Church
Weathercock about the suspicious-looking men
with coils of rope, wooden boxes and climbing
gear who had landed secretly last night in a
nearby cove.

'Egg-snatchers. I see danger for Golden Eagle,
who is sitting on four lovely eggs in a nest high
up the mountain,' said Witch sadly. But she and
Weathercock and their friend the sleepy
Weathervane Dragon wouldn't let the villains
steal the eggs without a struggle, even if it meant
flying up and down the mountain all day.

This exciting and entertaining new story for
young readers is by the author of *Magic at
Midnight*, which is also published in Young Puffins.

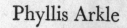

Phyllis Arkle

Magic in the Air

Illustrated by Mike Cole

Puffin Books

Puffin Books, Penguin Books Ltd, Harmondsworth, Middlesex, England
Penguin Books, 625 Madison Avenue, New York, New York 10022, U.S.A.
Penguin Books Australia Ltd, Ringwood, Victoria, Australia
Penguin Books Canada Ltd, 2801 John Street, Markham, Ontario, Canada L3R 1B4
Penguin Books (N.Z.) Ltd, 182–190 Wairau Road, Auckland 10, New Zealand

First published by Hodder & Stoughton Limited 1978
Published in Puffin Books 1980
Reprinted 1981 (twice), 1983

Typeset, printed and bound in Great Britain by
Hazell Watson & Viney Ltd, Aylesbury, Bucks
Set in Monotype Baskerville

For Samantha Jayne

Contents

Contents

1 Weathervane Witch flies off

It was very early morning. Sam, who worked at the farm just outside the small town, was walking past the school.

'People miss such a lot staying in bed half the morning,' he said to a bird which hopped fearlessly across his path.

Then he accidentally kicked something lying on the ground. 'Hello, hello, hello!' he cried. 'What's this?' He bent down and picked up a neatly designed broomstick, which he turned over and over in his hands. Then, puzzled, he glanced all round before he thought of looking up at the school roof.

His eyes brightened and a grin spread across his face. On top of the chimney, on a stand with four arms showing the points of the compass, wrought-iron Weathervane Witch held her position against the strong south-westerly wind.

'Ah, ha – I see,' called Sam. 'So you've dropped your broomstick? Tut-tut, very careless. But, never mind, Witch, don't look so worried. I'll bring it up to you.'

So saying, he tucked the broomstick under one arm, held on with the other, and shinned up a drainpipe. When he reached the guttering, he heaved himself up on to the roof. Then he started climbing up the sloping tiles. The wind switched course and pushed against the flat of his back.

'Thank you, wind,' panted Sam.

At last he stood on the ridge of the roof. Then, balancing carefully, like a tight-rope walker, he made his way to the chimney breast. He stood on tiptoes and held out the broomstick. The witch bent down and Sam placed the broomstick in her out-stretched hand.

'There you are, Butterfingers,' he cried cheerfully. 'Hold on to it a bit tighter, there's a good witch.' With a nod and a wave, he turned to go down again. Weathervane Witch fixed her eyes on Sam as he climbed down. Clever lad – she knew well that he had a great deal more knowledge of things that really matter than some people thought he had.

Just as Sam reached the ground, the school-house door opened and out came Mr Robson, the headmaster. Avoiding the man's eye, Sam busily brushed himself down. 'Just like him to come out now!' he murmured.

'May I ask what you were doing on my school roof, Sam?' said Mr Robson.

'Well ... er ... it's like this, Mr Robson, sir – Weathervane Witch's broomstick had fallen to the ground, so I carried it back to her, that's all.'

The headmaster said nothing, but he stared hard at Sam.

'You see, sir, she can't fly without her broomstick. It's magic! She can't do *anything* without her broomstick.'

'Really, Sam!' exclaimed Mr Robson. He glanced up at the weathervane and shook his head. 'Magic broomstick, indeed! You should know better. Be off with you, my boy, or you'll be late for work, and that's not like you – you were always on time for school.' He went quickly into the house and shut the door behind him.

Sam shrugged his shoulders. People missed a lot, not believing in magic. He waited just long enough to watch Weathervane Witch, her long straggling hair spread over her shoulders, hitch up her billowing black skirt and fly off on the broomstick.

'It's an unusual time for her to be in the air,' said Sam, thoughtfully, as he continued on his way. 'Still – no one's

about in the town yet, except me. She'll be back soon, no doubt. I guess she's going along to see Church Weathercock.'

He was right.

As Weathervane Witch flew over the rooftops of the small Scottish town that nestled in the valley, she could see ahead of her the moors leading to the mountain. She knew that in the distance were other mountains. When Witch drew in a deep breath, she could smell the sea from the east. It was a lovely morning to be out and about.

South-west Wind pushed against her, 'Whoosh! Whoosh! Whoosh!' it sang.

'Hey, not so hard,' cried Witch. 'You're blowing me off course.'

The wind laughed and the broomstick, with a defiant jerk, headed towards the church again. Weathercock, steady against the wind, was perched right on top of the tall church spire. When he noticed the witch approaching, he started to preen himself. He fanned out his fine copper-coloured wings and shook his beautiful curved tail feathers.

'Good morning, Weathervane Witch,' he said politely as the broomstick came to rest in the air beside him. 'I don't often have the pleasure of an early morning visit from you. What's on your mind?'

Weathervane Witch stroked her pointed chin, screwed up her beak of a nose and batted her eyelids thoughtfully, before she spoke. 'North-east Wind coming in from the sea last night noticed two men in an old diesel launch, acting suspiciously. Wind said the men landed in a quiet cove not far from here. They had coils of rope, climbing gear and wooden boxes . . .'

'Wooden boxes! Don't tell me. I know – to put wild birds' eggs in. The egg-snatchers are at it again, same as last year, are they?' Weathercock flapped up and down on his stand in indignation. 'They'll send the eggs to egg-collectors overseas and get a lot of money for them. What are you going to do about it, Witch?'

Witch ignored his question and gazed northwards to the mountain. She stared and stared until Weathercock's patience was nearly at an end. Then she said sadly, 'I sense danger for Golden Eagle, who is sitting on four lovely eggs in a nest, high above Dragon's Cave.'

'Dragon's Cave? So there's a dragon up there? Well, well, perhaps *he* could help to foil the robbers.'

Witch shook her head. 'Haven't seen *him* around for centuries,' she said.

'Pity . . .'

Witch's eyes roved over the rooftops. Suddenly she sat up straight and nearly fell off her broomstick. 'But we have a dragon – of sorts!' she cried.

Weathercock jumped. 'Where?' he whispered.

'On top of the town hall, of course.'

Weathercock bent his head to look down on the town hall on the opposite side of the square. 'What! Old Weather-vane Dragon?' he cried. 'You're not serious, Witch. Mind you, I've always been very fond of him, near-neighbour as he is but, really, he couldn't burn even a fly on his tongue, let alone frighten a couple of nest-robbers.' Weathercock shook his head in disgust.

'Mind you don't fall off your high perch – giving yourself airs,' said Witch. 'Come on, let's go across and have a word with Dragon, before the town wakes up.'

Weathercock followed Witch and settled beside her on the town hall roof. Looking up at the tall stout pole, Witch hissed, 'Psst! *Psst!*'

A forked tongue hung out of Weathervane Dragon's mouth. He yawned and showed two rows of pointed teeth. Then he stretched out his long, scaly body, clenched his sharp claws and flapped his bat-like wings.

'Just look at him,' muttered Weathercock.

Dragon glanced down. 'Oh! It's you, Weathervane Witch – and Weathercock! Goodness 'grac– I mean, good morning,' he said. 'Can I do anything for you?'

'Yes you can,' said Witch, firmly. Rising on her broomstick, she spoke to Dragon.

Dragon stifled a yawn now and then, and shifted on his stand as he listened. 'Oh, dear! Oh, dear! Poor Golden Eagle,' he sighed. 'How terrible! I'd like to help, really I would, but I haven't flown off my stand for, well, let me think, dozens – no, perhaps a

hundred years or more – I've lost count.'

'Well, it's time you had some exercise. It will be good for you. In fact, you'll enjoy it,' said Witch. 'We'll call for you this evening. I will have thought out a plan by then.'

'Do a few press-ups and hand-stands when no one is looking,' suggested Weathercock.

Dragon groaned.

Weathervane Witch pointed the broomstick in the direction of the school, while Weathercock flew back to the church. Dragon felt very uneasy, but he soon settled down and fell fast asleep again as the wind held him in position.

The little town woke up, and no one – except Sam, of course – knew about the early morning magic in the air!

2   At the old hut

That evening as Sam went past the school on his way home, a thick mist came down and covered the rooftops.

'Funny,' said Sam. 'I could have sworn it was going to be a fine evening.' He stopped and cocked his head to one side as he listened to a swishing sound above him.

'Well – what a surprise! Witch is off again. *Twice* in one day. Whatever's going on? Hope everything's all right.' He had a sudden thought. 'It's Saturday tomorrow. I'll be able to go out on the moors. Witch often goes there. Something interesting might be taking place, you never know.'

As Sam hurried home, Weathervane Witch, hidden by the mist, flew to the town hall. There on the roof she found Weathercock waiting for her. Peering through the mist they could see Weathervane Dragon asleep on his stand.

'Surely we can manage without *him*, Witch,' said Weathercock.

'I'm afraid not. He's going to be very useful – I hope.' Witch fumbled in the folds of her skirt and drew out a small bottle. Then she flew up to Dragon.

'Open your mouth,' she ordered.

Dragon opened his eyes.

'Your *mouth*, silly!'

'Why?' Dragon noticed the bottle and shrank back on his stand. 'Oh, no, please – I don't like medicine – nasty, horrid stuff. Never take it myself.'

'It isn't medicine. Come on, or else . . .'

'All right, if you insist. Anything to oblige,' said Dragon. *He* wasn't going to risk annoying Witch. She might mutter a spell, wave her broomstick at him and turn him into – what? A fly, or a toad, or a *mouse*? He shuddered, screwed up his nose and closed his eyes before opening his mouth.

'Wider!' cried Witch. She took hold of his snout and poured liquid from the bottle down his throat.

'Gulp, gulp, gulp . . . Enough! Oooh! Schlup!' sighed the beast.

'Manners!' cried Weathercock from below.

Then, suddenly, Dragon sat up smartly. He raised his head and stuck out his forked tongue. Steam came from his nostrils as he beat the air with his small wings.

'You can count on me,' he said. 'I'm ready for anything.'

Weathercock gazed at him in astonishment. 'Would you believe it! He looks like a new dragon. What's in that mixture, Witch, besides adders' stings and deadly nightshade?'

Witch ignored him. 'Now, listen to me, both of you,' she said. 'The mist has promised to stay around the town until we return. Follow me, and keep your eyes and ears open for anything unusual.'

'Where are we going?' asked Weathercock.

'Just to have a good look around and at the same time give Dragon a little flying practice.'

Off flew Witch, followed by Weathercock, then Dragon. To his surprise, Dragon was enjoying himself. When they had left the town behind them and were over the moors, he snuffed and sniffled loudly as he breathed in the scent of the gorse. He tilted his head to listen to bird song all around. After a while, he began to pant and lag behind his companions.

Suddenly, Witch pointed with her long skinny finger. 'I can see Dragon's Cave, high up on the mountain,' she cried.

Weathercock felt a cold shiver run down his back. Perhaps the dragon *was* up there. A fierce beast. Not like Weathervane Dragon. Weathercock glanced back at his friend. Poor old chap – he looked rather like a bumble-bee, with a wing-span too small for his body. He waited for Dragon to catch up with him, then flew alongside. 'You're flying quite well. The exercise will do you no end of good,' he said encouragingly.

The ground rose steeply beneath them. Glancing down, Weathercock noticed a small building half-hidden in a clump of trees.

'What's that, Witch?' he cried.

'What? Oh, that – it's only a derelict climbers' hut.' Then, without warning, she turned, bumping into Weathercock, who bumped into Dragon.

'Oh, don't mind me!' said Weather-cock.

'Nor me,' added Dragon, who was beginning to flounder.

'I'm sorry,' said Witch, 'but I'm glad you drew my attention to the hut, Weathercock. I wouldn't consider it a good hiding place, but the thieves might have camped in there for the night be-fore making an attempt to steal the eggs. We'll go and investigate – quietly, please.'

Dragon tried to stop puffing and blow-ing and started wheezing instead. 'Ssh!' warned Witch.

They settled on the roof of the hut and Witch put an eye to a small hole in the timbers. 'I can see two rough-look-ing men,' she whispered. 'And ropes, and an axe – and boxes! Just as Wind described.'

Soon a faint voice could be heard inside and Witch took her eye from the hole and put an ear there instead. Weathercock hopped about impatiently until Witch put a finger to her lips. Dragon began to yawn as he clung to the roof. 'He'll need another dose soon,' said Weathercock to himself.

'They're listening to the weather report on a radio,' Witch told them. Soon there was a click as the set was switched off. Then all three on the roof could hear the men talking.

'So it's going to be fine tomorrow,' said one.

'Yes, and there'll be no mist We'll start the climb straight after breakfast tomorrow morning.'

Witch turned to her companions. 'You heard?' she said. 'Very useful information. Now we've just time for a quick visit to Dragon's Cave and a peep at the nest, before we return to town for the night.'

She put up a hand to straighten her pointed hat, lost her balance and nearly fell off the roof. The little broomstick clattered to the ground. 'Oh, horror! My stick! My stick!' she moaned. 'Sam's right. "Butterfingers", that's me.'

Weathercock swooped down quickly, picked up the broomstick in his strong beak and returned to the roof with it.

'Here you are, Witch,' he said

urgently. 'Hurry! We'd better be off before we're seen.'

Too late.

The door of the hut was flung open and out ran the men. Weathercock turned to Witch. She wasn't there, but a curlew, its long curved bill pointing downwards, hovered overhead. Weathercock glanced quickly at Dragon. The beast was hesitating like a swimmer afraid to take the plunge. Weathercock rushed at him, gave him a good push and – off flew another curlew!

My turn next, thought Weathercock, lifting his wings in readiness for flight. But by then the men were looking directly up at him. 'Oh, dear!' muttered Weathercock as he flew off the roof, still *himself* – not a curlew.

He could hear the men shouting to one another, 'Just look at that rare, magnificent bird!'

'I've *never* seen such a strange, beautiful creature. What a sheen on its wings! Catch it – catch it. What a pity, it's getting away. We'll have to look out for it tomorrow and go all out to capture it . . .'

The men's voices faded as Weathercock flew up into the blue sky. His lungs were bursting as he went on and on and up and up, higher and higher, past jagged cliffs and rocks, until he landed on a jutting-out ledge. There sat two curlews, but, suddenly – hey, presto! – the curlews vanished and Weathervane Witch, broomstick and all, and Weathervane Dragon stood beside him.

'Fancy leaving me stranded like that,' grumbled Weathercock. 'I might have been caught, and then who would have taken my place on the church spire? The winds would be very sorry to lose me, if no one else would.'

He folded his wings and squatted down with his back to them. 'Giving me the fright of my life!' he added, shaking himself.

'Now, don't make a fuss, please, Weathercock,' said Witch, 'You were *seen*, which meant I couldn't possibly weave a spell right in front of the men. Do be reasonable.'

Weathercock hunched his shoulders.

'I'm very sorry you had a fright,' went on Witch, 'but it's given me a stupendous idea.'

Weathercock turned round. 'Oh, well, in that case – glad to have been of some use after all,' he said. 'Let's hear about the idea.'

'All in good time. All in good time,' said Witch. 'First, a little practice for Dragon.' She turned to the beast. 'In you go,' she said.

'In where?' said Dragon, startled.

'Into Dragon's Cave – there, behind you. I'm fairly certain there's no one at home!'

'It's a very small hole for a *dragon*,' said Weathercock.

'Oh, this is a sort of back door to the cave of the mountain dragon,' said Witch. '*His* entrance is on the other side of the mountain.'

Weathervane Dragon put his snout

inside the cave opening, blinked rapidly and shook his head. 'Ooh! You're not getting me inside that dark, nasty, smelly hole. There might be mice in there.'

'Mice! Did you say, mice? Don't tell me you're afraid of *mice*!' cried Weathercock.

Dragon shuffled. 'Hm. Well ... I don't mind beetles or spiders – quite like them – and even snakes, occasionally, but when it comes to mice. Ugh!' He shivered.

'Get in,' ordered Witch. She started to move towards Dragon.

'Oh, all right. All right. Don't make a scene,' grumbled Dragon as, with difficulty, he squeezed backwards into the small opening and lay down pant-ing, with his head and shoulders sticking out. 'Will that do?' he asked crossly.

Witch rubbed her hands together gleefully. 'Fine, fine,' she cried. 'That's *your* first task tomorrow, Dragon. Remember – to get into the cave and await my orders.'

'But he wouldn't frighten a mou–' began Weathercock.

'Stop putting your beak into my business, please,' shouted Witch, stamping her foot. She turned to Dragon again. 'You can get out now.'

But – sooner said than done. Dragon did his best. His tongue darted in and out like a rattlesnake's, and his ears waggled as he struggled to free himself.

'He must have got fatter all in a

minute,' said Weathercock, as he hopped around anxiously.

Witch took hold of the dragon's ears
and pulled and pulled, but she couldn't
budge him one inch.

'Turn him into something small,' suggested Weathercock at last.

'You just can't resist putting your
beak into my affairs,' said Witch. 'Of
course it's well within my powers to
make him smaller, but I intend saving
up my potions and spells for use tomorrow. We don't know what emer-
gencies might arise.'

She paused, then snapped her fingers.
'I've got it!' she cried. 'Dragon can
stay here all night, then he'll be ready,
right on the spot. He'll also be spared
the journey to town and back. The mists

will keep his stand in the town covered.'

'What! Stay here all night? By myself? No fear,' cried Dragon, as he started struggling again.

'But you can sleep s – l – e – – e – – p' said Witch, soothingly.

'Oh, well – I hadn't thought of that,' said Dragon. He laid his head down on his front paws and went to sleep.

Just then a bird with a strongly hooked beak and great talons soared above the crags. 'There goes Golden Eagle,' said Witch, as the great bird turned slowly in the air. 'The nest is tucked away to the right of us, behind those sharp rocks.'

Weathercock glanced at the sharp-edged rocks and shivered. He didn't envy anyone the climb up those rocks.

He followed Witch as she started the journey back. It was almost dark when they reached the town. Weathercock settled on his high perch and trembled with excitement when he thought of what might happen tomorrow.

The moon came from behind the mountain and he thought of Weather-vane Dragon snug – or half-snug, at least – in the cave. But whatever would his friend do if a mouse ran over his back? Weathercock chuckled and waited impatiently for morning to come.

3 Sam on the moors

Sam left the house very early next morning. He wasn't going to risk being sent out on errands this Saturday. There might be more important work for him to do. So that he wouldn't go hungry, he put some biscuits and a slab of chocolate into his pocket.

He ran past the town hall, glanced up at the roof and stopped when he saw the empty vane. 'Goodness gracious! Look at that!' he exclaimed. 'Sooner or later someone will notice old Dragon's missing – unless the mists

come down in time, of course.'
Across the square, he could see Weather-cock in position on top of the spire. 'Thank goodness you're still on duty,' he cried.

He set off across the square and turn-ed into the empty street leading to the school. At the school he looked up at the roof and checked that Weathervane Witch was on the vane. Sam went closer and bent his head backwards to see her more clearly.

'You can't fool me, Old Witch,' he called. 'I *know* there's something afoot. I'll be on the moors if you want my help.'

Witch made no sign.

'You heard me all right,' said Sam.

He left the town and soon turned off

the road, following a rough track which led on to the moors. There he stopped to watch a herd of deer moving slowly down a hillside towards the river below. He went on, but soon halted again. There was so much to see and examine! An ant-hill under a juniper bush; hares, their white winter coats turning to summer brown, leaping and darting about. Sam felt like jumping and skipping. There was magic in the air today.

He looked down at the town which was now covered in mist. 'I knew that would happen!' cried Sam. He was about to move on when he noticed two specks flying towards him. When they were directly overhead, he waved excitedly. The broomstick, with Witch astride, swooped down and circled for a few moments before rejoining Weather-cock.

Sam watched them as they flew off. He had been right, there *was* something mysterious going on. He was glad Weathervane Witch had seen him.

Sam had never climbed the mountain as far as Dragon's Cave. He had no intention of facing the dragon which he believed lived up there. Now he decided to go as far as the old hut.

When he entered the small wood which surrounded the hut, he stopped and sniffed, raised his head and sniffed again. Sure enough a delicious smell of frying bacon tickled his nose. He crept through the trees and glimpsed two men bending over a fire. Through the open door of the hut Sam could see climbing equipment – and wooden boxes! The lad clenched his fists and dug his fingers into the palms of his hands as he ran away, back through the wood and on to the open moorland.

Now he understood Witch's problem. Most likely these were thieves after Golden Eagle's eggs. Out on the open moor he saw, below him, a figure approaching. What luck – it was Mr Robson. As the headmaster drew nearer, Sam hailed him, 'Mr Robson, sir!'

The man stopped, looked up and waved. Sam sat down to wait, and eventually Mr Robson joined him. 'Well, Sam,' he said cheerfully. 'Enjoying a day out on the moors?'

'Yes, well, perhaps not *enjoying*, sir. Well, yes, in a way I am – but it's most

exciting. You see, there's trouble brew-
ing . . .'

'Trouble? What sort of trouble?'

The words tumbled out. 'Two men
with wooden boxes, egg-snatchers . . .
Weathervane Witch and Weathercock
are on the mountain by now, and I
don't know where Weathervane Dragon
is, but I think he must be up there

46

somewhere . . . and I don't know how to help but Witch knows I'm here. I'll just have to wait . . .'

'Now, now, Sam, it's too early for strangers to be on the moors and, in any case, if you have seen anyone acting suspiciously, the police ought to be informed –'

'But they never listen to me!'

'– and Weathervane Witch and Weathercock, and Weathervane Dragon are I'm sure, safe on their stands pointing the direction of the wind as usual.'

'Oh, no, they're not,' said Sam, looking down. Mr Robson followed his glance, saw the mist-covered town and frowned. He stroked his chin thoughtfully and murmured, 'The weather report said there'd be no mist about today.'

Sam laughed. Then he pointed excitedly and cried. 'Why, sir, here come Weathervane Witch and Weathercock on a reconnaissance.'

'Where?' cried Mr Robson, startled.

'There!' said Sam. But, even as he spoke, a small cloud shut the creatures from view for a moment, and then out flew . . .

'Two curlews!' exclaimed Mr Robson as he watched the birds circling overhead. 'Really, Sam!'

'But Mr Robson, sir . . .' began the young man, very put out.

'Now, Sam, you enjoy your day off and leave me to continue my walk across the moors. See you this evening, perhaps, on my way back.'

'Oh, well, if you're not climbing the

mountain today there's no need for me to remind you to beware of the dragon in Dragon's Cave, is there?' said Sam.

'That's an old wives' tale!' Mr Robson smiled as he set off again.

Sam sighed. He couldn't help it if no one believed what he told them. It was their loss not his. Just then two brown birds, beautifully streaked and patterned, swooped down and circled his head.

Sam waved his arms at them. 'You're too clever by half, Old Witch,' he cried. 'Making me look silly!' With a dip of their wings, the birds flew away.

Sam stood for a while enjoying the stillness. Then he heard voices. There was no peace! This Saturday the moors seemed almost as busy as the main street in the town. Who could it be this time? The men from the hut, perhaps. Sam thought it might be wise to hide, so he hastily crept behind a convenient bush. As luck would have it, just when two men came abreast of him, he sneezed twice! Immediately the footsteps halted and a man stepped round the bush and hauled Sam out.

'Oh, ho!' he cried. 'What do you think you're doing? Hiding from us?'

'It's Saturday,' said Sam, as he tried to wriggle free, 'and I'm going for a walk and doing a spot of bird watching at the same time.'

'Hm. Well – so long as you're not looking for trouble.' The man released Sam and said more pleasantly, 'We're on a climbing expedition.'

His companion joined in, 'By the way, if you're a bird watcher, have you seen an unusual bird round here – one with a marvellous sheen on its wings, sort of copper or bronze, with a beautiful, fanning-out sort of tail, which turns to a lovely green when the sun shines on it?'

'A very strange bird, indeed,' added

the first man. 'We'd like to captu– No, no, *no* – I mean we'd like to photograph it.'

Sam thought hard. He couldn't remember ever seeing such a bird on 'his' moors. Were the men pulling his leg?

But no. 'Come on, young man, think. It's a large, heavy-looking creature with fierce, beady eyes and must be exceedingly rare. It flies well enough, but rather stiffly.'

Large, flies stiffly, coppery-bronze or green? Sam shook his head slowly. 'No, I'm sure I've never ...' Then something clicked in his mind, and he put his hand to his mouth to hide a smile.

'Ah, yes, of course,' he said, when he had stopped smiling. 'I've often seen that particular bird – every day in fact – it sits on top of our church spire.'

'On top of the church? That bird? Rubbish!'

'Why, here he is back again – as himself!' cried Sam, as he spied the two weathervane creatures high above him. 'There, behind Old . . .' Sam stopped just in time.

'Behind Old – who? Where?'

When the men looked up at the sky there was no sign of the creatures, for they had dipped out of sight behind the trees near the hut. Sam shook his fist and muttered to himself, 'First weathervane creatures, then curlews, back to weathervanes again . . . You're making me feel dizzy as well as silly, Old Witch – AND I very nearly gave you away!'

'Stop muttering. We've had enough

of this nonsense,' said one man impatiently. 'We'll have to get a move on. There's a difficult and dangerous climb ahead of us.'

'There is,' agreed Sam. 'Many climbers have come to grief on our mountain. And I must tell you to beware of the dragon in Dragon's Cave.'

'What dragon?'

'Why! The one that's lived on the mountain for thousands, perhaps millions of years.'

'An old wives' tale!' they scoffed.

'That's exactly what Mr Robson said,' cried Sam.

'Oh, did he? Well, whoever Mr Robson is, he was right.'

'Come *on*. Save your breath,' interrupted the other man urgently. 'We'll need all our strength if we're to reach the eagl–'

'Ssh! Ssh!' Both men glanced sideways at Sam.

Sam scowled as he watched them depart. Then he cheered up. After all, the men might not even reach the nest, and if they did, well, Weathervane Witch would be able to deal with them.

Sam had always known better than to interfere when a witch had a job in hand, but – he looked in the direction taken by Witch and Weathercock – should he follow the two weathervane creatures? Perhaps it would be wiser to stay where he was.

Then he became more excited and decided he'd go along and see what they were up to. Just *watch* and not interfere. He wouldn't wait a minute longer. Sam leapt to his feet and ran off towards the hut.

4   Through the bog

Sam entered the wood. Rooks circled above him and he had to shake his head and wave his arms to ward off the flies. Soon he came in sight of the hut and, for the second time that morning, peered round a large tree trunk. There was no sign of Weathervane Witch, but in the sunlight something gleamed on the roof.

'My word – Weathercock!' murmured Sam. 'He's keeping a look-out, I suppose, but, silly bird, he hasn't even noticed me.'

Suddenly Witch appeared round the side of the hut. She glanced through the window before making for the door. At that very moment Sam heard a faint sound behind him. Startled, he knelt down quickly and put his ear to the ground. Sure enough he could detect not one, but *two* sets of stealthy foot-steps. The men must be returning! Had they forgotten something or, worse still, had they followed Sam to the hut?

No time for dallying. Sam rushed headlong out of the shelter of the trees. 'Danger, Witch – men approaching!' he yelled.

With her hand on the door latch, Witch swung round when she heard Sam. Then, quick to get the message, she beckoned urgently to Weathercock, mounted the broomstick and flew straight at the tall trees. The wind parted the branches and she disappeared from view. Surprised, Weathercock stood still and watched her go. Then he looked down at Sam.

'Shoo! Shoo! Get moving,' cried Sam, 'You're a sitting target up there. Witch is getting careless. She should have turned you into a curlew again.' He glanced quickly over his shoulder. 'Tell her I'll whistle *twice* when all's clear.'

With a flip-flap and a scurrying of his wings, Weathercock followed Witch just as the men burst into the clearing. They caught hold of Sam and shook him angrily.

'Just as we thought – you're up to something,' cried one. 'You were giving

59

a warning and I saw a green streak disappearing into the trees. It's that rare bird and you've scared it away.'

'You've been deceiving us,' the other man broke in. 'Come on now, we'll stand no more nonsense, show us where the bird nests.'

'But I've already told you, it lives on top of the church,' said Sam.

'If we believed that, we'd believe anything! Now, listen to me, you're going to lead us to the nest, or we'll . . .'

Sam shrugged his shoulders. 'All right,' he said at last. 'Follow me.'

'No more deception,' warned one man.

'And get a move on,' added the other. 'We've got a job to do on the mountain.'

'I know you have,' muttered Sam.

He led the way through the trees and into the sunshine. Across the moor, on and on they went.

'How much further?' shouted one man.

'Not much,' replied Sam, without stopping.

The ground became very squelchy and the men's feet dragged in the mud. They had difficulty in keeping up with Sam.

'Hey – wait for us!' they cried.

Sam stopped and turned round. 'Take care,' he shouted. 'Follow *exactly* in my footsteps or you'll fall into the bog.'

Sam knew which tufts of marshy grass were firm enough to hold the weight of a youth or a man and he led the men safely through the slimy ground. Pant-ing and blowing they heaved sighs of relief when the ground underneath their feet became dry and firm again. Sam waited for them to catch up with him. Then he pointed down the hillside.

'There!' he said.

'Where?'

'Where? I can't see anything.'

'Down there in the mist. That bird always – or nearly always! – sits on top of the church in the middle of the town.'

The men rushed at Sam. 'Think you're very clever, bringing us on a wild goose chase, don't you?'

'We'll see about . . .'

But Sam didn't wait to see about anything. Laughing, he ducked sideways and jumped like a deer as he made his way safely back across the bog.

Behind him he could hear the men shouting.

'Come back! Come back! We can't cross the bog without you.'

'No, you can't,' cried Sam.

'And it will take us much longer to climb the mountain from this side of the bog.'

'Yes, it will,' shouted Sam. He reached firm ground and waved cheekily at the men as he hurried off at full speed. He must give Witch the all clear as soon as possible. Then, if he didn't get in the way, perhaps – only perhaps – he might actually see her weaving a spell or doing something equally mysterious and exciting. She must have a very good reason for going to the hut.

At the hut all was peace and quiet-

ness. Evidently Witch was waiting for Sam's signal before she emerged from the trees. Sam pursed up his lips ready to whistle – when he thought he heard footsteps. Not again!

He had no need to put his ear to the ground this time, for the footsteps could be clearly heard. Feeling thoroughly exasperated, Sam quickly hid behind a

bush. He waited until he heard someone entering the clearing. Then he peeped round the bush, leapt to his feet and
rushed out. 'What a relief! I'm glad it's
only you, sir,' he cried.

Mr Robson jumped. 'Why, Sam, you
did give me a fright,' he said. 'I heard
shouting coming from this direction,
so I turned back to investigate.' He

opened the door of the hut and took a quick glance inside. 'Nobody in there. Come on, Sam, tell me what's going on.'

'Well, sir – such excitement! Weathercock was keeping guard on the roof – at least he thought he was, but he didn't see me – and Weathervane Witch was just about to enter the hut when the two robbers came creeping up.'

'Really, Sam. I've *told* you . . .'

'I'm glad I was here to give the alarm,' went on Sam. 'Witch has a lot on her mind at present, and she's not taking enough precautions. The men are intent on stealing the eggs, but they've also caught a glimpse of Weathercock. They want to capture him as they think he's a very rare bird –

which he is, of course, if you see what I mean, sir.' Sam laughed.

But Mr Robson said nothing for a while. 'Now, Sam,' he began at last. 'Where are those men you keep talking about?'

'Oh, they're on their way up the mountain by now from the other side of the bog, but, don't worry, Weathervane Witch will be after them in good time. She'll protect the eggs somehow.'

Mr Robson looked up at the empty roof. 'And Weathercock?' he said.

'He's hiding in the trees with Witch,' said Sam.

Mr Robson straightened his shoulders and stared hard at Sam. 'Listen to me, Sam,' he said. 'There's *no* witch up here and *no* cock – except hundreds of grouse on the moors, of course – and as for men . . .'

'But Mr Robson,' cried Sam. 'I've seen them *twice*, and . . .'

'That's enough, Sam. When *I* see Weathervane Witch and Weathercock flying about, and two men about to steal wild birds' eggs, I'll believe you, but until then I suggest you join me in a walk across the moors.' Mr Robson strode off. 'Come *on*, Sam,' he cried.

What bad luck, thought Sam. Perhaps he'd never have another chance of watching Witch at work. They'd only walked a few yards when Sam turned round, cupped his mouth in his hands and gave two loud whistles.

'Good heavens, Sam!' cried Mr Robson, looking back over his shoulder. '*Must* you do that?'

'I promised I'd give the all clear,' said Sam.

'Will you never learn to be sensible?' sighed Mr Robson.

Sam followed the headmaster through the wood and on to the moor. Then he started to dawdle and soon fell behind.

'Don't loiter,' called Mr Robson briskly. He waited for Sam to catch up with him. 'We'll climb the mountain as far as Dragon's Cave, if you like – the air and exercise will do you good.'

'Oh, not me, sir,' said Sam firmly. 'I'll stay here and rest for a while.' He lay down on his back, put his hands behind his head and looked up at the

69

white puffy clouds drifting across the blue sky.

Mr Robson gazed down at him. 'All right, Sam, have it your own way,' he said. 'I'll go for a walk on my own.' Suddenly he laughed and his eyes twinkled. 'But I'll take your advice and keep away from Dragon's Cave.'

'Very wise, sir,' said Sam. 'You'd be surprised what trouble you might run into up there.'

'Nonsense, Sam,' said Mr Robson as he walked away.

'"Nonsense", always "nonsense",' whispered Sam. He crossed one leg over the other and swung his foot in the air. He decided to wait only until Mr Robson was out of sight, then *nothing* would stop him running back to the hut.

He stared up at the mountain. Was the Mountain Dragon in his cave? And where was Weathervane Dragon hiding? Although it was a warm day, Sam shivered with excitement and anticipation. Only another minute, a quick dash back to the hut, and perhaps *this* time he would see Witch at work.

5 Weathercock to the rescue

Weathervane Witch had heard Sam's whistle as he walked away with Mr Robson. She turned to Weathercock, who was perched on a nearby branch. 'It's safe now,' she said. 'Back to the hut. I've got the beginnings of an idea.'

'No use asking what it is, I suppose,' said Weathercock.

'No,' said Witch, as they landed outside the hut. 'You stay outside and keep guard – *properly* this time.' She lifted the latch, opened the door and stepped into the hut.

Weathercock took up sentry duty outside the door. His head jerked to left and to right and this time his bright eyes missed nothing. Then from inside the hut came a most eerie noise which went on and on and on. Weathercock pecked at his shoulder to make sure he was awake, and not dreaming on his stand on top of the church!

He took a quick peep inside the hut. To his surprise, he saw Witch riding round and round on the broomstick, about a foot from the floor, chanting to herself all the time.

She noticed Weathercock. 'Keep out! Out!' she yelled as she balanced on the broomstick. 'You'll be caught in the spell if you're not careful and that would spoil everything.'

73

Weathercock retreated and waited outside until the chanting ceased and Witch sailed through the open doorway.

'I've tried out a new spell and I think it will be very successful,' she said, obviously delighted with her efforts.

'Another dark secret?' said Weathercock as they rose into the air.

Witch turned to glare at him. The broomstick jerked to one side and the hem of Witch's cloak caught on the top branch of a tall pine tree and – would you believe it! – the broomstick fell down, down through the branches, right to the ground. Witch hung upside down from the branch, looking for all the world like a piece of washing, or a kite caught in a tree.

'Oh! Oh! Oh!' she squealed.

'Quick, Weathercock, get my stick. I'll be hurled to the ground any minute, and the blood's already rushing to my head. Quick! Quick!'

'All right! All right! Don't make such a fuss,' said Weathercock, all in a twitter himself. 'Butterfingers,' he said under his breath as he fluttered to the ground and began searching. Nowhere could he see an iron broomstick.

'Oh, my goodness!' he murmured, as he continued the search. He thought of Weathervane Dragon alone on the mountain and of the men climbing up to the nest. 'This is certainly no time to be dilly-dallying looking for a broomstick!' he cried.

'Get a move on,' shrieked Witch, her voice becoming muffled as a playful wind picked up an edge of her cloak and blew it across her face.

'I can't find it anywhere,' called Weathercock. 'It's like looking for a needle in a haystack. What on earth shall I do? Wait a minute – ah, thank goodness, here it is, stuck between two boulders.'

He put his beak into the cleft and tried to reach the broomstick. He poked about until he could stand it no longer. 'Ough! Ouch! My beak!' he cried.

'Never mind your beak,' croaked Witch. 'Help! I'm slipping.'

'It's impossible – I can't reach it,' cried Weathercock, dismayed. 'Now what?'

Witch's voice came in faint gasps, 'Then go and get Sam.'

As it happened Sam, having watched Mr Robson out of sight, was already on his way back to the hut. In less than a minute he appeared in the clearing. Hearing a rustling above his head, he looked up. Did his eyes deceive him, or could that possibly be Weathervane Witch hanging upside down from the highest branch?

'Good heavens, Witch,' he called, unable to restrain a smile. 'Where's your broomstick?'

Witch pointed at the boulders. Weathercock flew into the trees as Sam raced across. In no time at all he had the situation well in hand. He rolled up his sleeves, put an arm down between the rocks and groped with his fingers until he felt the iron. Then he drew out the broomstick and waved it at Witch.

With the broomstick tucked under one arm, he started to climb the tree. He stopped to rest at intervals. 'Phew!' he cried. 'Don't do this too often, Witch. It's much more difficult than climbing a drainpipe.'

When he reached the top branch, he stretched out an arm and handed the broomstick to Witch. 'If this goes on, I'll have to get you a roll of sticking plaster so that you can stick your broomstick to your hand. And just look at that great tear in your cloak – careless!'

Weathervane Witch and Weathercock waited at the top of the tree until Sam was safely on the ground.

'Don't worry, Witch,' said Sam. 'You've plenty of time as I delayed the

men crossing the bog.' Sam was disappointed that he hadn't seen Witch weaving a spell, but at least he *had* helped her.

Witch mounted the broomstick and, followed by Weathercock, flew back to the mountain. They kept well out of sight of the two men toiling up the steep slope. As they approached Dragon's Cave they heard a funny rumbling sound which echoed round the rocks.

Weathercock started. 'Whatever's that, Witch?' he whispered. 'Perhaps the real dragon has come out of his cave?'

'Don't be silly!' cried Witch. '*I've* guessed what it is.'

At last they reached the ledge in front of Dragon's Cave – and there was

Weathervane Dragon, fast asleep and snoring loudly. 'I thought so! He never misses an opportunity to fall asleep,' said Witch, as she prodded the beast with her broomstick.

'Snort! S – n – o – – r – – t,' breathed Dragon. Witch poked him again, hissing indignantly, 'Come on, wake up,

you lazy, good-for-nothing beast. Stop that hideous noise.'

'Ouch!' cried Dragon. Then, opening one eye, he saw Witch. 'Oh, sorry, Witch,' he said. 'I was just having a snooze while I waited. I'm wide awake really.' He straightened up and tried to look alert. 'Ready, Witch,' he said.

'Well, I'm not ready yet,' said Witch. She lay down by Weathercock, who was peering over the edge. The men were getting nearer. Witch glanced up at the eagles' nest. 'I'm thankful we're here,' she said. 'The eagles are away foraging for food and the nest is unprotected.'

Weathercock was tense with excitement. Even Witch seemed jittery, as they watched and waited. The men were now on a steep outcrop of rock directly underneath the nest. They would soon be able to snatch an egg, perhaps two eggs – perhaps all four eggs! Weathercock shuddered.

'It's time, isn't it, Witch?' he said nervously.

Witch nodded. 'I'll attend to Weathervane Dragon before I hide behind that large rock near the cave opening. In the meantime I want you to . . .'

'Oh, that's all right. I've guessed all along what you want *me* to do . . .'

'Clever of you.'

'I'm to entice the men away from the nest on to this ledge, and then leave everything to Weathervane Dragon.'

'That's the idea,' cried Witch. 'Give

me a signal – crow twice – when it's time for me to give Dragon the potion. Ready? Off you go – make sure you don't get caught.'

'Caught? Not me!' said Weather-cock. He stood poised on the edge for a moment, and then flew off towards the eagles' nest.

6　The dragon in the cave

Weathercock felt lonely as he swooped low over the nest. Below him, the men were too busy climbing up the steep rocks to look up. A strong wind came along and buffeted the villains. Weathercock felt better, for a friend was at hand.

Weathercock watched carefully. One more foothold, then a handhold, and the nest would be in real danger. A man reached up – now! thought Weathercock.

He crowed very loudly. Then, swift

as a rocket, he darted down and narrowly missed the man's head before he rose again and flew back to the ledge.

The man looked up startled. Then he cried excitedly, 'It's that rare bird again. Keep an eye on it.'

'We must go after it *now*, before it disappears again,' shouted the other man. 'Come *on*, we might never get another chance. The eggs must wait.'

They started to move slowly and cautiously towards Dragon's Cave, while Weathercock, in full view, strutted about on the ledge. When the men were directly under the ledge, he crowed twice.

Behind him, Witch turned to Weathervane Dragon. 'Now then,' she said. 'There's no time for argument.

Look smart – open your mouth – wide!'
Dragon parted his teeth and let the
liquid trickle down his throat.

'It's a double spell,' Witch told him.
'First, you'll shrink a little, so that you
can get out of the cave, then you'll
swell up, like a balloon, and become
very large and fierce-looking. After that,
well, it's up to you. Do your best – be
bold, fearless, terrifying!' She disappeared behind a large rock.

A man's head appeared over the
ledge, and an arm shot out. 'Got him!'
yelled a man, triumphantly, as Weathercock was grabbed by the tail.

Weathercock struggled and looked
round anxiously for help. Where was
'fierce' Weathervane Dragon? Surely
the silly creature hadn't run away?

Then, to his amazement, he saw a reptile, like a small lizard with wings, scuttling towards him. The creature's tongue darted in and out and it spat and squeaked as it ran. The man didn't even notice it.

Heavens! What a catastrophe! Witch has bungled everything, thought Weathercock. We're all lost. Why – he's as small as ... as a *mouse*! The man tightened his grip and Weathercock fought to free himself. I'm going to be caught after all. Oh, I wish I knew what to do – how could Witch have made such a stupid mistake?

Still holding on to Weathercock, the man scrambled on to the ledge. But, at that very moment, a terrible noise was heard. It seemed to come from *inside* the mountain. Weathercock stopped struggling as the man let go of his tail, and little Weathervane Dragon stood still aghast. It came again – much louder this time – a shattering sound which seemed to shake the rocks. Then a flame, red and glowing, and another and another, shot out of the cave mouth.

The man crouched down and covered his head with his hands, while Weathervane Dragon flew off the ledge after Weathercock. The other man, who had been following his companion, peeped over the ledge. 'Wha . . . what's going on?' he asked, fearfully.

'I . . . I . . . I don't know, but I think it must be that dragon the young man spoke about.' Another flame darted out. 'Look out!' he cried.

He sprang back, lost his balance and fell off the ledge on top of his friend. Somehow they managed to scramble to their feet and went slipping and stumbling and running down the mountainside. Behind them the roaring grew louder and louder, until it seemed to them that the air all around was filled with the noise and the glow from the flames.

When the flames had died down, Weathervane Witch, looking very shaken, crept from behind the rock. She was soon joined by her two companions. They had to shout to make themselves heard.

'I think someone is at home after all,' yelled Weathercock.

'Yes,' said Witch, 'and not too happy

at being disturbed. Hurry! He might come round from the other side of the mountain. We'll leave him in his cave to sleep for another hundred years or so.'

As they took to the air, Witch said, 'We must give the old dragon his due – those ruffians have had a fright they'll never forget.'

'*I* did my best,' said a very small voice.

'Of *course* you did, Weathervane Dragon,' said Weathercock. 'Witch shouldn't have made you as small as a mou–'

'That's enough, Weathercock,' said Witch. 'He'll be quite all right soon. I gave him the wrong mixture, that's all. Anyone – even a witch – can make a mistake. See, he's growing already. Let's hear no more about the matter.'

Weathercock had the last word. 'Giving him the wrong mixture! Dropping your broomstick all over the place! What next?'

While all this was going on, Sam stood on the moor and looked up at the mountain. He watched the flames and the smoke and covered his ears when the roaring became deafening. When there was a lull, he glanced round and saw Mr Robson striding towards him. Sam ran to meet him.

'Mr Robson, Mr Robson, sir, *did* you see the red glow on the mountain? It was much better than bonfire night. And did you hear the roaring?' He jumped up and down in excitement. 'Something's happened up there, all right. The dragon's been in action!'

Mr Robson stopped. 'Why, Sam, that was just a very heavy roll of thunder, following forked lightning –'

'Thunder! – that noise?' exclaimed Sam. 'I'm telling you, it was the old mountain dragon. Fair roused, he must have been.'

Sam looked up at the sky. 'And here are the weathervane creatures on their way home.'

Mr Robson followed his glance. 'Three curlews!' he cried.

'They may appear to be curlews, sir,' said Sam. 'But, believe me, the one in front is Weathervane Witch, then Weathercock, with Weathervane Dragon – I've been wondering where he'd got to – bringing up the rear. Witch tore her cloak earlier on. What will she do about that?'

Sam wheeled round. 'And here come the two nest-robbers I told you about this morning.'

The men stumbled towards them. 'Run – run for your lives,' panted one. 'There's a terrible dragon up there. We heard it. It might be following us . . .'

'. . . and flames poured out of a hole in the rock. We might have been burnt alive. Run, run, run –'

'But I told you to beware of the dragon,' Sam shouted after them. 'Serves you right for not believing me.' He watched them sprinting in the direction of the hut, and laughed. 'They'd win any race going at that pace!' he said.

Mr Robson looked bewildered. 'I must admit you appear to be right about the robbers, Sam. I noticed what they were carrying in the rucksacks. We're wasting time. You run off back to town and alert the police, while I go along to the hut and try and detain the men. Tell the sergeant I sent you. We must make quite sure these men never return.'

'They'll never want to come back here,' cried Sam. 'I expect they've gone to pick up their camping gear, and then they'll be off.' Sam ran, full pelt, towards the town. When he arrived at the police station, he found Sergeant Wilkins in charge.

'Now then, Sam,' said the sergeant. 'You can see I'm busy. What's on your mind?'

'Trouble on the mountain, sir,' said Sam. 'I don't know for sure what's happened, but Weathervane Witch has –'

'Weathervane – who?'

'Weathervane *Witch* from the school. With Weathercock and Weathervane

Dragon she's somehow – I'm certain she has – saved Golden Eagle's nest from being robbed. The thieves have rushed off to the hut to collect their things.'

'Now, steady, Sam. Calm down. In the first place, I'm quite certain the winds would have something to say if their weathervane creatures started to caper about all over the moors. As for nest-robbers – well, we've been keeping a look-out and we haven't heard or seen any strangers about. So just go quietly off home, Sam, in case your mother's getting anxious about you.'

'But Mr Robson's gone after the men, all on his own. *He* told me to come to you.'

'Mr Robson, did you say? Oh, well,

that's different. Let's go.' Sergeant Wilkins left a colleague in charge and followed Sam out of the town and on to
the moors.

'Hurry, sir,' called Sam as he led the
way. He did not stop to look at the deer
on their way back from the river, or to
watch the hares or the birds.

'Hurry! Hurry!' he cried.

7   Mr Robson on the roof

Sergeant Wilkins was out of breath by the time he and Sam came in sight of the hut. Mr Robson was leaning against the door post.

'Have they managed to escape, Mr Robson?' called Sam.

The headmaster grinned. 'Escape? Dear me, no!' he cried. 'Good afternoon, Sergeant. Come and look inside but, take care, don't step across the threshold.'

The two men were standing as still as statues in the middle of the floor. Sam thought they looked silly. 'Why don't they move?' he asked, puzzled.

'Because they can't raise their feet from the floor,' said Mr Robson. 'Don't ask me why they can't, because I don't know.'

Sam scratched his head as he thought hard. 'I saw Old Witch near the hut earlier on,' he said slowly. Then he snapped his fingers. 'I've got it! She must have worked a spell on the floor. The men might just as well be *glued* to it.'

Mr Robson and the sergeant exchanged glances. 'If that's the case, Sam,' said the sergeant, 'have you any suggestions for releasing them?'

'Oh, don't worry. I'm sure the spell will work itself out, now we're here.

Look! It's beginning already. They're able to lift their feet a bit.'

The men tried hard to move forward but without much success at first. 'What's happened to us?' moaned one. 'It feels as though I've got leaden weights tied to my ankles. Can't you do something?'

Mr Robson and the sergeant shook their heads, but Sam cried, 'Keep trying!'

The men groaned as, inch by inch, they managed at last to raise their feet and walk very slowly, like two old men, as far as the door.

'Well, now you're able to walk, you can accompany me to the police station,' said the sergeant briskly. 'You'll have a bit of explaining to do.' He glanced at the rucksacks. 'I wouldn't be at all surprised if you are the culprits who stole protected birds' eggs last year.'

Free from the pull of the floor, the men made a dash through the door, but the sergeant, helped by Mr Robson, stopped them in time.

'It's useless trying to escape,' said the sergeant. 'We'd soon catch you again.' He laughed. 'And Old Witch might join in the chase – they wouldn't get away from *her*, eh, Sam?' He patted Sam's shoulder. 'Anyway, joking apart, I must thank you for doing some useful work today.'

'Oh, don't thank me,' said Sam. 'It's all due to Witch and Weathercock – and Weathervane Dragon, of course; I mustn't forget him.'

The men scowled. 'The boy talks nonsense,' said one.

Sam ignored him. 'The mist has disappeared from the town and you'll find they're all back on duty, pointing the direction of the wind. No need to worry about them.'

The sergeant started off with the two men.

'They've left their belongings in the hut,' Sam called after him. 'Shall I bring them to the police station?'

'Don't worry, Sam,' was the reply. 'Thank you, but I'll send someone to examine the hut and collect anything essential.'

Sam and Mr Robson stood in the doorway. 'I must say it was very clever of Witch to trap the men like that,' said Sam. 'She must have guessed they'd come back here before making for the coast.'

Mr Robson raised his eyebrows and looked at Sam. 'There must be a perfectly ordinary explanation for the men being unable to move,' he said. 'They probably picked up a sticky substance on the soles of their boots as they fled down the mountain, and when they came to stand in the hut –'

'Nonsense!' cried Sam.

'Sam!'

'Sorry, sir, but I suggest you go inside and see if you can find a trace of anything sticky on the floor.'

Mr Robson moved forward slowly a step at a time, testing the floor surface. Sam watched from the doorway. 'It's all right, *you* won't get stuck,' Sam told him.

Head bent, the headmaster continued the search. After a time he straightened up and said, 'Well, Sam, there's nothing to be gained by staying here the rest of the day.'

Sam followed him from the hut, across the moor towards the town. Once he looked back at the mountain. Everything seemed as quiet and peaceful as one would expect on a calm, warm spring evening.

'I forgot to tell Sergeant Wilkins about the mountain dragon's part in this,' he said. 'But, no matter, he wouldn't have believed me.'

'He would not,' said Mr Robson firmly.

106

As they entered the square, Sam glanced up at the town hall roof. 'There's Weathervane Dragon back on duty, just as I said he'd be,' cried Sam. 'I must admit he looks a bit jaded, but that's understandable after his efforts. And look at Weathercock over there, as sprightly as ever.'

Mr Robson glanced up at the church spire. 'He's *always* there, Sam,' he said.

As they approached the school, Weathervane Witch could be seen on the roof. 'Well, she looks in good shape,' said Sam, 'except for that tear in her cloak – by jove, you can see the sky through it! She's on duty. Oh, no she's not all right – where's her broomstick? Good gracious, would you believe it?

Like a woman losing her umbrella all the time. Now where can that broomstick have got to this time?'

'Tut-tut, Sam,' sighed Mr Robson.

Sam started to search up and down the pavement and along the gutters. 'Hope it hasn't fallen down a drain.' Sam was beginning to worry. Mr Robson pretended not to join in the search, but he followed Sam.

'What's this?' said the headmaster suddenly, as he bent down and picked up a neatly designed broomstick lying in the road.

'Oh, *there* it is, sir. Thank you – what a relief. Give it to me, please, and I'll climb up to the roof with it.'

'Oh, no, Sam. You're not going up there again.' Mr Robson held on to the broomstick. 'In any case, there's no need. This rod is only a piece of iron from a railing or something.'

'Oh, no, sir, it isn't –'

'Off you go, Sam. No more arguing.'

Sam walked away slowly. Turning a corner of the building, he leant against the wall and waited for at least two minutes before he peeped round. The sight which met his eyes made him want to laugh aloud!

With the broomstick tucked under one arm, Mr Robson had started climbing the drainpipe. When he reached the roof he stopped to get his breath back. Then, very carefully, a short, slow step at a time, he edged along the ridge. When he reached the chimney, he solemnly held out the broomstick.

Weathervane Witch bent down and took it from him without a word.

But Mr Robson cried, 'Old Witch! I'll have to see about having that tear in your cloak repaired.'

Sam hugged himself with delight. He watched as Mr Robson made the difficult descent, hurried into the schoolhouse and shut the door firmly behind him. Sam was so used to people not believing what he told them that he smiled to himself all the way home at the thought of Mr Robson on the roof handing the broomstick to Witch! Mr Robson would probably ask the blacksmith to mend the cloak, but how would he explain to the man how Witch managed to tear the garment?

*

That night, a strong wind sprang up unexpectedly and Sam couldn't get to sleep. It wasn't a nasty, whining wind, but a jolly I'm-out-to-enjoy-myself sort. Eventually, Sam crept out of bed and went over to the window.

In the light of the full moon, he could clearly see the church and the spire, but he couldn't see Weathercock for he wasn't there! Sam pressed his nose right on to the glass and gazed at the stars.

Suddenly he heard a familiar swishing sound and Weathervane Witch flew past the window. Her torn cloak streamed out as she steered her broomstick towards the moors. Behind Witch came Weathercock, his feathers gleaming like silver in the moonlight. Weathervane

Dragon lagged behind the others, until the wind gave him an extra push and he surged forward.

What a wonderful sight! Sam hoped Mr Robson was watching from his own bedroom window. Were they all going to join Golden Eagle, to celebrate the success of Witch's plan?

Sam longed to go with them. With Witch at hand, to say nothing of Weathercock and Weathervane Dragon, Sam thought he might summon up enough courage to take a peep at the mountain dragon in his cave – provided the fabulous beast had really gone to sleep again. And perhaps Golden Eagle wouldn't object if he just had a quick glance at the four eggs, snug in the nest. (Later on, what a thrill it would be when, out on the moors on a Saturday, he would catch a glimpse of four eaglets on the wing.)

Sam peered through the window until all he could see of his friends were three specks in the distance. Then he rubbed his cold nose and got back into bed. He was well content that he had played a small part in saving the eggs. He had no doubt that tomorrow Witch, Weathercock and Weathervane Dragon would be back on their vanes, turning at the will of the winds.

In future, Sam intended keeping a close watch on Weathervane Witch, for there was no knowing what she would get up to next!

Other Young Puffins by Phyllis Arkle

Magic at Midnight

Wild Duck had stood motionless on his inn sign for 200 years or more, but the night he heard of the midnight magic he stiffly flapped his wings and came down to try the world.

The Village Dinosaur

The cranes had lifted something extraordinary out of the quarry – a real dinosaur, and it seemed to be waking up! Jed Watkins wanted to keep it in the village as a pet, but the stuffy Parish Clerk wanted to get rid of it before it did any damage.

Two Village Dinosaurs

Two dinosaurs spell double trouble as Dino and Sauro trample their amiable way through the village, causing chaos and confusion on every side.

Some other Young Puffins

Carrot Tops

Joan Wyatt

Fifteen stories of everyday events like making a jelly, growing a carrot-top garden, visiting Granny – all tinged with the make-believe that young children love.

The Worst Witch

Jill Murphy

Mildred Hubble is the most disastrous dunce of all at Miss Cackle's training school for witches. But even the worst witch scores the occasional triumph!

A Gift from Winklesea

Helen Cresswell

Dan and Mary buy a beautiful stone like an egg as a present for their mother – and then it hatches into the oddest animal they ever saw!

Tell Me a Story
Tell Me Another Story
Time For a Story
More Stories to Tell

ed. Eileen Colwell

Stories, verses, finger plays for young children, collected by one of the greatest living experts on the art of children's storytelling.

Stories for Under-Fives

Stories For Five-Year-Olds

Stories For Six-Year-Olds

Stories For Seven-Year-Olds

More Stories for Seven-Year-Olds

Stories for Eight-Year-Olds

Stories for Nine-Year-Olds

ed. Sara and Stephen Corrin

Celebrated anthologies of stories specially selected for each age group and tested in the classroom by the editors.

Grimblegraw and the Wuthering Witch

Barbara Sleigh

Prince Benedict and Princess Yolanda are captured by the giant Grimblegraw, who has been enchanted by an evil witch. They must find her and trick her into lifting her spell.

Adventures of Sam Pig

Sam Pig and Sally

Sam Pig Goes to Market

Sam Pig Goes To The Seaside

Yours Ever, Sam Pig

Sam Pig at The circus

Alison Uttley

Five sets of comical stories about Alison Uttley's best-loved character, who always tries to be helpful.

Who is he?

His name is Smudge, and he's the mascot of the Junior Puffin Club.

What is that?

It's a Club for children between 4 and 8 who are beginning to discover and enjoy books for themselves.

How does it work?

On joining, members are sent a Club badge and Membership Card, a sheet of stickers, and their first copy of the magazine, *The Egg*, which is sent to them four times a year. As well as stories, pictures, puzzles and things to make, there are competitions to enter and, of course, news about new Puffins.

For details of cost and an application form, send a stamped addressed envelope to:

The Junior Puffin Club
Penguin Books Limited
Bath Road
Harmondsworth
Middlesex UB7 0DA